SISKA GOEMINNE

MEREL EYCKERMAN

NO ONE ELSE LIKE

you

WJK WESTMINSTER
JOHN KNOX PRESS
LOUISVILLE • KENTUCKY

In this world there are more than seven billion people
crawling in the grass, like little ants.
They walk around, sit down, think of things, then jump up again.
They run from here to there and there to here.

Some of them know why they are running.
Others have no idea at all—they just go with the flow.

People live in tall towers in the city or in a cottage in the field,
where the wind is always whistling.
Some people live on a mountain way up high, on a boat on a river,
in a tent in the desert, or in the dark, dark woods.
You can even find them in places where it is hard to live:
where the earth is scalding hot or the water icy cold.

Some people try to do a thousand things at once.
They work, make phone calls, drive around,
send emails, and watch the television in the evening.
Only at night, when the moon has come up, are they finally quiet.
But some of them are even noisy in their dreams . . .

People have strange things on their bodies:
a button on the belly, lobes at the ears, and dots on the nose.
They have fingers that can push, grab, pinch, and cuddle.
They also have a head. Every once in a while, they use it to think!

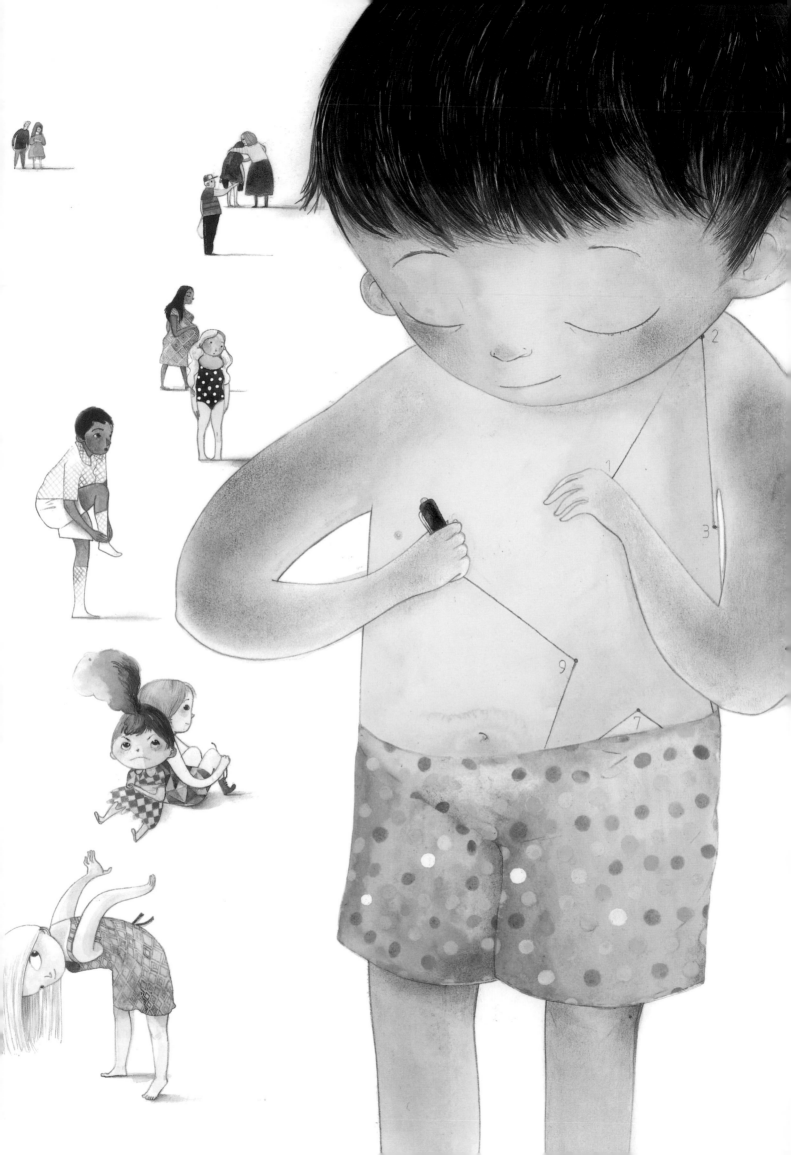

People come in different colors, shapes, and sizes.
There are people with wiggly toes or skinny legs,
with freckles in summer and goosebumps in winter,
with short arms or very long ones
that can reach anything.

People wear everything you can imagine:
shoes with flowers or with wheels, a coat of wool or nothing on their arms,
short pants or a long dress.
They carry boots or backpacks or cell phones, and each other, now and then.
Some of them love hats, caps, masks, or veils.
Others want their head bare in the rain and in the sun.

Some people want to be different from everyone else,
and others like to be alike.

People are fragile.
You shouldn't drop them, because they might fall to pieces.
They love a little care: food and drink,
but also hugs and sympathy.
Or pay them a compliment—that makes them glow inside.

Some people are always happy,
even when it rains cats and dogs
or when their favorite book is lost.
Others seem to have a gloomy cloud
that follows them wherever they go.

Some people are born scared.
They shiver when it gets dark,
stay away from roller coasters,
tremble when a dog approaches.
Others walk a tightrope while whistling a song,
climb a steep mountain or parachute out of a plane.
They seem to be afraid of nothing and no one.

Some people like to roar.
They think it sounds better than a whisper.
There are people who sing about all the beautiful things to come,
and others who tell stories about the mysteries of the past.
People like to say, "I love you"
and like to hear it even more.

Some people get lost in their own family.
They have lots of brothers and sisters, nephews and cousins,
aunts and uncles all over the world.
They sometimes wish for a little spot of their own.
Others live with their mom or dad,
or with one small granny.
They sometimes dream of a big, big family
as a cozy circle around them.

People believe in different things: Many people believe in God.
Others believe in secret powers, Santa Claus, or the beams of the moon,
in daisies and cows, in a heaven full of stars, or in nothing at all.
Some believe in themselves, for a start.

There are nice people, smart people,
stubborn people, cranky people,
funny people, and scary people.
There are people who like reading
on their belly in the dew and people
always wanting something else and something new.

Most are angry when they lose
and proud when they succeed.
They are sad when someone dies
and glad when they are loved.

Seven billion people
like little ants in the grass.

But not one of them is just like you.

For you, Staf. The dearest, the funniest, the wisest—the YOU for me.
—Siska

I know who is the YOU for me—it starts with a B.
—Merel

Original title: *Jij, tussen vele anderen*

This edition published 2017 in the United States of America by Westminster John Knox Press, 100 Witherspoon Street, Louisville, Kentucky 40202-1396. Online at www.wjkbooks.com.

17 18 19 20 21 22 23 24 25 26—10 9 8 7 6 5 4 3 2 1

BOOK DESIGN
Dries Desseyn

COVER ILLUSTRATION
Merel Eyckerman

LIBRARY OF CONGRESS CATALOGING-IN-PUBLICATION DATA
Names: Goeminne, Siska, author. | Eyckerman, Merel, illustrator.
Title: No one else like you / Siska Goeminne ; illustrated by Merel Eyckerman.
Other titles: Jij, tussen vele anderen. English.
Description: Louisville, KY : Westminster John Knox Press, 2016.
Identifiers: LCCN 2017023877 | ISBN 9780664263539 (printed case : alk. paper)
Subjects: LCSH: Individual differences--Juvenile fiction.
Classification: LCC PZ13 .J49513 2016 | DDC [E]--dc23 LC record available at https://lccn.loc.gov/2017023877

PRINTED IN CHINA

Most Westminster John Knox Press books are available at special quantity discounts when purchased in bulk by corporations, organizations, and special-interest groups. For more information, please e-mail SpecialSales@wjkbooks.com.